darkest DEVOTION

devotion series

PERSEPHONE AUTUMN

PERSEPHONE AUTUMN

BETWEEN WORDS PUBLISHING LLC

Abstract Passion

<u>Novellas</u>

Reese

Penny

<u>Lake Lavender Series</u>

Depths Awakened

One Night Forsaken

Every Thought Taken

<u>Stone Bay Series</u>

Broken Sky — Prequel

<u>Standalone Romance Novels</u>

Sweet Tooth

Transcendental

<u>Poetry Collections</u>

Ink Veins

Broken Metronome

Slipping From Existence

PUBLISHED UNDER P. AUTUMN

<u>Standalone Non-Romance Novels</u>

By Dawn

To the introverts with an inner vixen…
It's playtime!

ONE

ELLA

"Come out," she said. "It'll be fun," she said.

Naomi. My best friend. The girl who bends anyone to her will. Including me. And although I know her ability to sway decisions, I fall for her pleas every single time. Sales is in her blood, whether it is cars at her father's car dealership or last year's wardrobe to the desperate-to-be-cool freshman class—well, now sophomores.

Somehow, Naomi convinced me to tag along to some mysterious underground club. The kind of "club" that is never in the same location twice. The kind you have to know someone to receive an invite. The kind you only tell trusted people about. Yeah, that is where we are.

Except this underground party is not just loud music, influential substances and gyrating bodies. *"It's like an old-school rave."* Lies. Bald-faced lies.

"What is this, Becky?" Her fake name rolls off my tongue in a hiss.

Naomi and I have been frequenting clubs since before legally allowed. Some guy she dated junior year knew someone who made fake IDs. We never used them to drink, only to get inside. For a year and a half, she has been Becky and I have been Hazel. Additionally, no guy ever gets our actual name. Less worry in the creepsters department.

She spins to face me, trying her damnedest to hide her wicked grin. "I swear." Naomi holds up her right hand. "I had no idea."

I roll my eyes. "Your cheeky smile says otherwise."

"Swear." She dons a more serious expression. "But it is funny."

What the hell is funny about walking into a room that basically looks like a porn studio?

By no means am I a prude. Walking in blind to a secret party thinking it is music and drinks and dancing is one thing. Walking in blind to a secret party and seeing sweaty bodies slapping skin while other people watch is a whole different ball game. More than anything, it just would have been nice to know.

Huffing out a breath, I shake my head and hook my arm in hers. "Fine," I grumble. "But you are stuck with me all night."

She jerks away and meets my eyes. Slams her tight fists on her hips. "No way."

"Afraid so." My lips tilt up in a wicked smirk. A smirk that vanishes seconds later.

"Alright then. You want me at your side all night." Her eyes roam the room until she lands on something that makes my insides twist. "Let's go."

If anyone hears this... save me, please.

When my best friend suggested we party to celebrate graduating high school, an elusive sex free-for-all was not what popped in my head.

One... who visits sex parties with their friend? No one, that is who. I love Naomi, but not on that level.

Two... what does she expect to happen? I easily picture her thinking it would be okay for us to go our separate ways and do our own thing while between these four walls. To spot a hottie and ditch me to hook up with him.

Too fucking bad. She should have given her plan more thought before dragging me into the unknown.

We reach the other side of the warehouse space and Naomi weaves us between a crowd. As they make room for us, two women on blanket-covered pallets come into view. It isn't obscene or grotesque. Actually, watching them pleasure each other has me clamping my thighs tighter. As weirded out as I was when we walked in the door, the sight of these women pleasuring one another has me entranced.

Too entranced.

Sexual preferences have never bothered me. I have always been more attracted to people for who they are, not the genitals between their legs. Naomi, on the other hand, has always given off the vibe that she is straighter than straight.

Looking to my left, I open my mouth to ask Naomi about her sudden interest in women. But… she isn't there.

You have got to be kidding me.

Not only did my best friend covertly lure me to a supersecret sex party. Now, she ditched me.

Super.

Fucking.

Shitty.

I pull my cell from my back pocket to text her, but I already have a message waiting.

Naomi: Sorry, E. A hottie was throwing signals.
Ella: You suck!

I can and can't believe she ditched me. She will grovel for weeks to come, I will make sure of it.

Winding my way through the crowd, I locate a makeshift bar and buy a bottled water. In the corner of the room, several tattered couches sit in a circle around another blanketed pallet bed. Thankfully, one couch remains unoccupied.

Parking myself on the couch, I sip my water and stare at the couple in the middle of the circle. A man, his pants shoved to his knees, sits leaned back, palms on the floor behind him. His erection thick and red and veiny. On her hands and knees, a woman bobs up and down his length.

Her skirt too short to cover her bare slit, and her top long since removed.

Much as I don't want to be here alone—hello, unwanted weirdos—I can't seem to make myself walk out the door. Tonight wouldn't be the first time I called a cab because Naomi found someone to hook up with. I shouldn't have expected tonight to be any different.

But this place is not like the other places we partied. Bars with nothing but drunks I can handle. This place is not that. Not by a long shot.

A man sits next to me on the couch and I stop breathing. He doesn't say anything, but I feel his eyes on my profile. The heat of his stare as he waits for me to look his way.

Why did I sit at the end of the couch? Damn it.

Minutes tick by and nothing happens. The guy sits next to me, eventually looks away to watch the woman giving a blow job, and squeezes his own cock through his jeans. Awkward as the situation is, at least he keeps his hands to himself.

A moment later, as if he heard my thoughts, his calloused hand rests on my thigh.

Fuck. My. Life.

TWO

THOMAS

W‍HEN THE GUYS from the firm invited me out to celebrate my birthday, I assumed we would hit up the corner bar, have a few drinks and some greasy food. Talk shit for hours, then go our separate ways. I did not expect to walk into a big orgyfest.

Soon as we passed the threshold, they gave a shoulder slap and wandered off.

Who the hell brings their coworker to a sex party? God, if the firm found out about this, they would probably reprimand us all.

At least they walked away. Don't get me wrong, I am all for bonding with coworkers. Just not like this. I prefer not to share my sexual predilections with business partners.

I wander through the industrial building, hands in my pockets as I avoid eye contact. By no means am I shy or pure, especially when it comes to sex. But I don't know this place, I don't know these people. And although I have tried many nontraditional things in the bedroom, I have yet to perform the act in front of others. So, for now, I keep my hands to myself while I survey the scene.

The space is dark, lit only by the occasional lamp or colored bulb. Sultry music from a portable DJ booth thrums and echoes off the walls like a concert hall. Sweat and sex and marijuana permeate the air. On occasion, an arm or hand brushes against my bicep, shoulder, or abdomen as I move through the crowd. And on every available surface, people are fucking.

Less than a minute after we walked in, my cock was harder than steel. With each step forward, my erection grows achingly painful. My balls thick and heavy and in desperate need of release.

"Fuck," I whisper to myself.

In a dimly lit corner, I sit on a couch facing a couple giving oral. The man faces away from me, but his head is tipped back in ecstasy while a woman sucks him off. Exhibitionism may not be my thing, but voyeurism is a whole different story.

The longer I sit in this place, the longer I hear and see and smell sex, the harder it is to hold back. The harder it is to restrain my hands.

My eyes scan the area. Look for anyone with eyes on me. My surveillance comes up empty and I sag deeper into the couch.

Unable to resist any longer, I unfasten my jeans and fist my cock beneath my briefs. Stroke my erection with a firm hand. Occasionally pinch the tip and moan at the sting it causes. Stroke after stroke, I bring myself closer to release, as the woman does the same for the man feet in front of me.

Then, I stop mid-stroke when my gaze shifts slightly.

Opposite me in the couch circle, a young redhead fidgets next to a man who put his hand on her thigh. I don't know them, don't know if they are together, but her body language screams for someone to rescue her. In this place, there are no heroes, just different levels of perversion.

For her, I may be the lesser of evils.

I fasten my pants, rise from the couch and saunter to where she sits. There isn't much time to come up with a plan of attack. The only option is to say the first thing that comes to mind. And since the man's attention has been solely focused on her and no one else on the couches, I play the easiest hand.

"There you are," I say as I step in front of her. Green-rimmed hazels peek up through a mess of red curls. *Fuck me running.* "Thought I lost you."

For a moment, confusion knits her brow. I extend my hand and widen my eyes a fraction. And then realization clicks in place for her. She slips her hand in mine and rises from the couch. It isn't until this moment that the man snaps out of his sex-induced fog.

"Hey, sugar. We were just about to have some fun," the man says, hand jerking his dick harder. He looks me up and down, then licks his lips. "The more, the merrier."

I tug her into my side and snake my arm around her waist. "Thanks for the offer, but we've already got something lined up. Another time."

The man shrugs off the proposition and eyes the remaining people in the couch circle in search of someone else to satisfy his urges. At least that went easier than expected.

Without hesitation, I lead her away from the couches and near a vacant section of wall. She spins to face me, a soft smile on her lips as she leans against the concrete. My first true visual of her up close.

Damn, she is enchanting.

"Thanks for the rescue," she shouts over the music.

I nod. "No problem. You looked a bit uncomfortable."

She laughs, and I love how it adds a glow to her aura. "Yeah, you could say that. Wasn't my idea to come here." She nibbles at her bottom lip. My eyes follow the action while my dick thickens behind my zipper again. "But I'm not a prude," she says in a rush. "That guy creeped me out, though."

"Same." I lean closer to her. Inhale deeply and detect a hint of peach. "About both." She doesn't shift away from my slight advance, doesn't take her eyes off mine, so I inch closer. "I'm Thomas. Hope I don't creep you out."

"You don't." Her shoulders lift and fall. "Hazel." She licks her lips and swallows.

My lips tug up at the corners. "Does everyone else believe you?"

The lines of her forehead deepen. "Believe me?"

"That your name is Hazel."

She swallows again. "It is."

I eliminate another inch between us. Brush the hair off her neck. Lean close enough to almost taste her skin. "I'll let it go for now." Her chest rises and falls in short bursts, her breath hot on my neck, breasts grazing my chest. "But I will know your name."

Reluctantly, I inch back. Gift her personal space back. Give both of us a moment to breathe.

I may not have come to this place intentionally, but the carnal energy here is off the charts and flooding my bloodstream. Lust fogs my thoughts, but so does she. Moans and whimpers mix with the music, and my cock begs for some form of relief.

Tonight isn't my first exposure to orgies. I dabbled in college. Fucked my share of women and sucked my share of men. But the way she surveys the room, I'd venture to guess this is her first time in such a setting. And fuck me, I want to show her how good it can be. I may not be an exhibitionist, but she makes me want to be.

"You come here with a boyfriend?" My fingers curl into a fist at the thought of her answering yes.

She shakes her head. "A friend."

Thank fuck.

"Are you seeing anyone?"

Another shake of her head. "You?"

"No."

Her frame relaxes as she licks her lips, and my only thought is I want to lick them too. Taste the sweetness of her lips. Feel the softness of her skin. Inhale her peachy scent for hours as I explore her flesh and mark her as mine.

I lean into her again. Press the straining bulge behind my zipper to her belly. She doesn't shift away or gravitate closer. So I cage her in. Invade her space fully. Drop my chin and run my nose along her jaw to her ear. Inhale deeply and groan.

"You'd make a beautiful pet," I say before sucking her lobe. With her curves and alabaster skin... fuck, she would stun me in leather.

She hums and I feel it in my groin. "Not sure if I should be offended" —she exhales against the hollow of my throat and I groan— "or turned on."

"Definitely turned on." My lips and tongue trail down her neck. "Want to get out of here, not-Hazel?"

A soft chuckle vibrates her throat. "Why leave the party?"

I freeze where her neck and shoulder meet. Slowly, I ease back to meet her gaze. For someone who cringed next to a man jerking his cock minutes ago, she seems more open than expected. Or am I reading her all wrong?

"Why indeed."

THREE

ELLA

STRIPPING bare before dozens of people is uncomfortable as hell and the most liberating thing I have done.

I'd said "why leave the party?" partially as a joke. Thomas asked me to leave with him and I had no clue what to say or do. Not as if I hadn't been abandoned by Naomi in the past and found a ride home. But tonight is different. Hooking up with someone after a sex party wouldn't be the same as leaving the bar and squeezing in a quickie in the back seat.

From the looks of it, Thomas is older. Not much; maybe early to midtwenties. His button-down shirt tucked in his jeans tells me he is not just some schmuck off the street, but not quite big league. He exudes confidence, but watches me as if worried I will run off.

Should I go?

He tosses my shorts next to my shirt, then looks up at

me as he kneels at my feet. And it feels so heady… having a man before me like this. Although I still wear a bra and panties, I feel the need to wrap my arms around my middle. To hide myself from passersby. What stops me? Thomas's wanton gaze as he stares up my body from below.

I lean on the wall for support. Let the concrete cool my fevered skin and settle my jittery nerves. Every other second, I remind myself to breathe. Remind myself everything will be fine.

Right?

I don't know this man, yet I let him peel away my clothes without a word, without an ounce of resistance. Yes, he rescued me from some old creepster on the couch. But what if he is some serial killer who preys on innocent —not that I am innocent—women and charms them with his sinful smile and wicked words?

Should I stop him? Should I push him away, put my clothes back on and get the hell out of here? Yes.

Is that what I am going to do? Probably not. Because right now, his tongue is slowly trailing up my thigh and all my rational decisions walk out the door.

"Such a pretty little pet." He licks along the seam of my panties, from the junction of my thighs to the edge of my hip. Fingers hook in the elastic band and slowly tug the thin material down my thighs. "So fucking pretty," he says at the sight of my bare mound.

Since he peeled off my top, I have yet to say a word.

Have yet to touch him. Not that I don't want to, it's just…
I don't know. Thomas overrides my brain. Short-circuits
my thoughts. Makes me question what I am doing
and why.

Sex is a good time. I get my jollies and go about life
when it ends.

But I have never exposed myself like this. Never made
myself so utterly vulnerable. Never let a man take off my
clothes in a warehouse full of people. And I have no clue
why I am now.

"Thomas, I…" I cover myself with my hands. Every-
where I look, eyes are on me. Watching. Waiting for more.
Touching themselves as they watch someone touch me. "I
don't think I…"

He rises from the floor and crowds my vision. Steps
into me and blankets me in his heat. Grips my chin
between his thumb and finger and directs my eyes to his.

"Hey." When my eyes avert to the small crowd, he
twists me back to his line of sight. "Ignore them." My
brow pinches at the middle. "Me, only look at me."

I open my mouth, objection on the tip of my tongue,
but don't get a word out. Thomas crushes my lips with his.
For two breaths, I freeze. Question what the hell I am
doing. Then I melt into him. Kiss him back. Moan when
he licks my bottom lip and parts them with his tongue.
Fist his shirt when he deepens the kiss. Haul him flush
with my frame and press into his groin.

He breaks the kiss and I smile at how ragged his
breathing is. At how much I affected this man. I may be

young, I may not have much life experience, but I can bring a man to his knees and make him breathless. If that isn't power, I don't know what is.

Reaching up, I unfasten the buttons of his shirt. Spread the cotton wide and stare down his chest. Slender without definition. A slight smattering a hair that disappears beneath his jeans. *That's a trail I plan to blaze.*

My fingertips trace along his skin and he sucks in a breath when I dip below his navel. Grabs my wrist and halts my touch.

"Keep that up and I'll embarrass myself before I fuck you." Before I complain how unfair it is I can't touch him, he drops to his knees, presses his nose between my thighs and inhales deeply. "So sweet, my pet."

The term "pet" should turn me off. Should make me fiery and argumentative. I am not a cat or dog. Not something you put on a leash and take for a walk. Not at your beck and call or someone you command.

But every time he calls me pet, I purr like a kitten. My pussy aches for him to say it again. To stroke me like the pet he says I am. Reward me like a good girl for being so wet.

As the crowd grows thicker, I keep my gaze fixed on Thomas. Watch as his hands trail up my calves, my thighs, and spreads them farther apart. Watch as he leans in and runs the tip of his nose from my bare mound to my clit. His tongue darts out and licks my slit. The rumble of his moan vibrates my flesh as he tastes me for the first time.

I want to fist his hair, shove him deeper between my thighs and grind against his face. I want to, but I don't.

Him, this place, these people… it is a fantasy exis-tence. What person wants more than sex with someone after being in a place like this?

Thomas is not the swine that sat next to me on the couch earlier, but he may not be much better. He still stripped me bare without asking permission. Still touched and tasted my skin without consent. And because I never said yes, my clenched fists ache to tug his hair and yank him back. Shove him to the floor and make him beg to touch what doesn't belong to him.

But I don't move my hands. Don't fist his hair. Don't push him away.

Because I love the feel of his tongue between my legs. Love the way his fingers bruise my hips and ass as he hauls me closer and fucks my pussy with his mouth. Love the way he groans against my flesh as he devours me whole. Love the way his eyes haven't left mine since his tongue licked my lower lips.

My legs quiver and knees threaten to buckle. Thomas tightens his hold on me. Cocoons my hips with his strong arms. Performs some magical exorcism on my clit with his tongue.

And then I free-fall into oblivion. Get lost in a pool of undiluted lechery.

Thomas doesn't slow his assault. If anything, he takes me harder. Captures my clit between his lips and sucks.

Hard. Draws out my orgasm and builds me up for the next.

Then, he releases me from his mouth. I wobble in place as he rises to his full height. Reach for him as he pulls his wallet from his back pocket. Shove his shirt down his arms as he undoes his pants and exposes his thick, swollen cock. Pout when I reach for his cock and he stops me.

My eyes lock on his and ask why. Why can't I touch him like he touched me moments ago?

"Not tonight, my pet." He strokes my cheek with his knuckles. "Tonight, I want to bury my cock in your pretty little cunt and never leave." Corner of the package between his teeth, he rips open the condom wrapper and rolls the latex down his length.

His shirt falls to the floor before he hoists me up. My legs wrap around his waist and arms around his neck. Pants bunched at his ankles, he staggers forward until his weight pins me to the concrete; the tip of his cock grazing my entrance.

Tongue darting out, Thomas licks up my neck to my ear. "You one of those girls that's quiet during sex, pet?"

I rock my head side to side. "Yes and no." He sucks my lobe between his lips. "Don't really spend time getting to know the guys I fuck."

He rears back as if I slapped him. And I swear he growls before responding. "We may have just met. I may have just feasted on your pussy. And we may be seconds from fucking. But that sure as shit doesn't mean tonight is it."

When I first looked at Thomas earlier, I never would have pegged him as the possessive type. The guy who *claims* his woman. If he were any other person, I would tell him to fuck off. Tell him he doesn't *own* me. That no one *owns* me.

The words are right there, on the tip of my tongue, but they refuse to be spoken. Because somewhere deep down, rooted in my bones, I like the way Thomas wants to assert ownership of me. Like the way he wants to command my pleasure.

If Thomas were anyone else, I would have left this place the moment I stood from the couch. But he isn't anyone else. And for some unknown reason, I want him more with each passing beat.

"Okay," I acquiesce, my voice fragile. "Not just tonight."

The tip of his cock teases my entrance. He rocks his hips slightly and the head dips inside. I gasp at the feel of him, at the way he toys with my body. Then he rears back, rocks forward and sinks deeper. My nails bite his skin as my thighs squeeze him tighter.

"So fucking tight." He runs his tongue over my lips. "Ever been with a real man, pet?"

Since the day I lost my virginity, sex has never been anything more than sex. Every guy I hooked up with was the same age as me, give or take a year, but all in high school. So, no, I hadn't technically been with a man.

I shake my head. "Never had the chance."

"Mmm," he hums against my lips. "Guess that makes us both lucky." My brow scrunches as I regard him. "Lucky me, because I get to be your first. Lucky you because you'll never want anyone else."

I open my mouth, ready to call him presumptuous, but the words never come.

Thomas rocks his hips forward and fills me to the hilt. I forget how to think or speak or care about anything but the way he feels inside me. "Oh, god," I moan out as my nails claw his upper back.

"Sweet fucking Christ." His hands on my ass grip tighter, spread my cheeks and guide me as he pistons in and out.

The crowd vanishes and the music fades. All I feel is the bass as it rattles the walls and Thomas's cock as it thrusts deep inside me. His jagged breath heats the skin beneath my ear. His sweat-slicked skin slaps me over and over as he drives us both to orgasm.

It all feels too much and not enough. The exhibitionism and vulnerability. The voyeurism and perversion.

I love sex—not that it has ever been this good—but it was always just an act. A means to an end. A way to get my jollies. But most of it happened in the back of a car, in someone else's bed or a random bathroom. It was fast and meaningless and I usually had to do most of the work if I wanted to get off.

With Thomas, sex is a new experience. The way he

speaks and acts and takes. He is both soft and hard, tender and aggressive, light and dark.

A hand snakes up my spine, fingers comb through my hair and curl into a fist, and then he yanks. A sting spreads over my scalp. His arm around my waist grips me harder. Holds me to him. Then his teeth pierce my skin where my neck and shoulder meet.

"Harder," I choke out.

He growls against my flesh as his hips piston faster. "Get there, pet," he commands.

I shut out everything but the unadulterated lust flowing through my veins. Let go of everything except him and me and how good we feel together.

He licks up my neck and sucks the spot beneath my ear. "That's it." Teeth clamp down on my lobe. "Come on my cock like a pretty little pet."

Stars steal my sight. White noise floods my ears. Thomas yanks my hair harder. Pumps his hips faster and hits me deeper as I ride my high. Then his teeth clamp down where my neck and shoulder meet. His hips stop, but his cock jerks.

As he loosens his grip on my hair, the room comes back into view. Countless people masturbate at the sight of us, but I no longer feel the need to hide my body. In fact, I want to watch. Want to join. Want to play.

Thomas kisses up my neck and along my jaw before taking my mouth. "My sweet pet." He strokes my lips with his finger. "Mine. Understood?"

My eyes dart between his, judge the seriousness of his

words. Because fucking me in a room of strangers is one thing. Claiming me as yours and no one else's… we will need to have a separate conversation about that. For now, though, I follow his lead.

"Ella." His brows pinch at the middle. "My name. It's Ella."

A wicked grin takes over his expression. "Indeed, it is, pet."

ELLA. Sweet and quiet, yet a firestorm in her own right.

Although she never said no, never pulled away from my advances, I questioned her consent from the moment we reached the wall and I invaded her space. I never asked permission to touch her, to kiss her, to fuck her, yet I took what I wanted anyway. It wasn't until she told me to take her harder that I truly gave over to the beast inside. That one word was all the permission I needed.

With our clothes back in place, I take her hand in mine and weave us through the crowd. An hour ago, I would have stopped and played the voyeur. Watched couples and trios and groups as they gave into their carnal nature. Now, all I want to do is leave this place with her.

Ella shivers as we step onto the sidewalk. At this hour, the warmer temperatures from earlier are nowhere to be found. I drape an arm over her shoulders and hug her to my side.

"Better?" She nods. "We're almost to the car."

"Where are we going?"

Great question.

When I pulled out of Ella and the lust bubble popped, reality crept its way back in. I wasn't embarrassed to fuck her in front of everyone. If anything, claiming her in front of a crowd turned me on more. But now, I wanted her all to myself.

"My place," I say as I unlock the car and open the door for her.

She hesitates getting in. "Uh…"

I step into her and twirl a lock of her brilliant-red hair around my finger. My lips a breath from hers. "Please, Ella." Closing the space between us, I kiss her. Brush my lips gently against hers. Revel in the buzz beneath my sternum as I connect with her in a way so different from before. I rest my forehead on hers. "I'm not ready to let you leave yet."

Her fingers trace down the buttons of my shirt. Fist the fabric and tug me closer. Lips drop back on mine and she controls the kiss. Slow and soft at first. But then her grip on my shirt tightens. Her tongue dives deeper. Explores further. A series of sweet whimpers spill from her lips and I devour each one.

It takes every ounce of willpower to break the kiss. Her groan of irritation makes me chuckle, and I kiss the tip of her nose.

"Please, Ella. Come to my place."

She leans back and holds my gaze. "Don't laugh, okay?"

I furrow my brow, then shrug. "Whatever you need to say, I promise not to laugh."

After a deep inhale, she licks her lips. "I know we just had sex in front of a bunch of people, which I was surprisingly okay with." She huffs out a laugh. "But this feels different."

"Going to my house?" She nods. "Why?"

Mentally, I prepare myself for some outlandish answer. Like I might be some serial killer who preys on young women, has sex with them in public, then lures them back to my place to off them. Or that I am some extremist with twisted fetishes I only perform in my own home.

I do like kink, but nothing involving blades or body fluids.

What I don't prepare myself for is her actual answer.

"I've hooked up with a lot of guys." I grind my molars and growl. Her lips kick up at the corners. "Mostly in public places, but not in the open." She pauses a beat. "On rare occasions, I'd hook up at someone's house. Parties or the random hangout that turned into more." I close my eyes and take a deep breath. Work to tamper down the heat in my veins. She flattens her palm over my heart. "What I'm trying to say is, there was never anything beyond the sex. No connection afterward. No desire for more." Her eyes momentarily drop to her hand, then lift to pin me in place. "With you… going to your place… it scares me."

"I scare you?" I ask in a weak voice.

She shakes her head. "No, not you." Her fingers toy with the button at the hollow of my throat. "More than sex with another person scares me. Meaning more to someone scares me."

My arms wrap around her protectively and hug her close. "It's okay to be scared. I am too."

"You are?" she mumbles into my chest. I nod. "Why?"

"Because I've never wanted anyone the way I want you." And I mean it.

Since losing my virginity the summer before high school, I've had a lot of sex. College was a blur of late nights, alcohol, studying and one-nighters. In the past decade, I had two serious relationships. By serious, I mean we were more than sex. We shared meals and went to movies and spent time together for months. One lasted three months, and the other lasted seven months. With both, they wanted more than I was willing to give at the time.

But I am not that person now. Although I like to have a good time, my priorities have changed. Work and rent, food and sleep rule my life. Going out tonight was an exception. And women... as much as I love sex, women have been on the back burner for weeks.

Ella is a deviation from the straight path I have been walking. A deviation I plan to follow and get lost on.

She smirks, then glances to the side. "What's so special about me?" she whisper-asks.

I grip her chin and steer her eyes back to mine. "Not

sure what it is, but I feel it here." I tap her hand still over my heart. "This odd twist in my chest. It hurts, but in a good way."

"Oh," she whispers.

"So, please… come home with me. I don't care if we crash the moment we walk inside. But I'm not ready to say goodbye. Not yet."

Her lips press to mine in a chaste kiss. "Okay, I'll go home with you." A bright smile lights up her face. "Just don't kill me in my sleep."

I laugh, then draw an X over my heart. "Promise."

What I didn't say was I want to keep her. That the need brewing inside me would never let me hurt her. Nor would I ever let anyone else hurt her. And I am a man of my word.

FIVE
ELLA

I WAKE to a palm on my breast and an erection against my ass. And for a moment, I don't know where I am. I don't move or take a breath.

The hand on my breast sweeps beneath the sheet and trails down my midline. Glides down my bare mound and dips between my folds. In and out, in and out. Then he swirls the slick digit over my clit and my breath stutters.

"So responsive."

Thomas.

He sweeps my hair off my neck, kisses between my shoulder blades, then licks up my spine. My moan in response is harsh and throaty and unladylike.

"And fucking perfect."

He wraps his free arm around my torso and pinches my nipple. I press my ass into him. Gyrate my hips and grind against his erection harder with each circuit.

"Pretty little pet. Fuck my hand. Come on my fingers."

He bites the skin beneath my ear. "And maybe I'll reward you."

Reward me? Not sure what that means, but every nerve ending in my body screams to be rewarded.

"Promise?" I ask as I rock my hips harder. Fuck his fingers with aggression.

He pinches my nipple harder and I whimper. "Only if you're a good little pet and do as I say."

His teeth sink into my neck. For two breaths, I feel nothing but the sharp burn. And then the burn fades. In its place is an ache for more. More teeth. More pain. More of him.

I reach around and palm his ass. Grind harder against his thick cock. Fuck his fingers as if my life depends on it. "I'll always be your good little pet."

He twists my nipple and my walls constrict around his fingers. I come on his hand, soak my thighs and the sheets. Cry out as he continues to pump his fingers in and out. And just before I tell him I can't take anymore, just before I beg him to stop, he pulls out his fingers and sucks them off.

"You are the sweetest little pet. I could spend my life between your legs and not get enough."

What if I wanted him to spend his life between my legs?

Turning around, I shove Thomas flat on the mattress and straddle his hips. Lean down and crush my lips to his. His fingers bruise my upper thighs as I rock my hips over his length. And as much as I want to ride him, I also want him in my mouth.

I break the kiss. Bite my way down his chin, his throat, his torso. Shuffle down the bed until I hover over his pulsing cock. Fist the base with one hand while I kiss the tip.

"Goddamn, pet. You're killing me," he groans out. His stare heats me from crown to heel as he gazes down at me. "Put my cock between those pretty lips." Fingers toy with my hair before he cups my cheek. "Take what's yours."

Fuck.

I have never been this wet. Never been with someone so possessive and commanding. On the street, those characteristics would be an automatic turnoff. In the bedroom, though… I want more.

My tongue darts out and I lick his tip. Taste his saltiness in my mouth. His fingers curl and fist my hair. His moans echoing off the walls. The pleasure I give him makes me heady. Puts a wicked grin on my face before I flatten my tongue at the base of his cock, lick up his shaft and take him down my throat.

"Sweet fucking Christ," he chokes out. He yanks my hair as his back bows off the bed. "You'll unman me in no time if you keep that up."

His words only encourage me further.

But after I take him again, his hands swoop under my arms and he drags me up his body.

"Hey," I protest. "Wasn't done."

"Tell me you're clean." The tip of his cock grazes my folds.

My brow lifts. "I am." Hands on his pecs for balance, I glide up and down the surface of his cock. "Are you?"

He fists my hips. "Yes," he bites out. "And I had a vasectomy years ago." I freeze, tilt my head and study him a beat. "Don't want kids. We can talk about it later."

I shake my head. "Not necessary." My hips rock as I dip to kiss him. "I get it."

Before he responds in turn, I line him up with my entrance and sink down. He grips my hips impossibly harder. Grunts as I claw his pecs and rock up and down his length. Curses as I fuck him faster, harder. Sits up, clamps down on my nipple with his teeth and punishes my body until I climax.

Still in the haze of my orgasm, he flips me onto my belly, hikes my hips up, slaps my ass and slams back into me. He paws my ass, spreads my cheeks and growls as he fucks me relentlessly. A thumb presses my puckered hole and I groan.

"Has anyone touched you here?" His thumb circles the hole; adding more pressure every other circuit.

"No," I pant out.

"Good." Moisture slides down my crack and he uses it to lubricate the puckered entrance. A burning sensation consumes my hole and I stop breathing. Thomas bends over me and kisses my neck. "Breathe, Ella."

Although I love it when he calls me pet during sex, my name on his tongue while we are this intimate is potent.

Intoxicating. An all-new brand of arousal. And I want to hear it more. Daily, and often.

With a deep breath, my body melts into his touch. "Such a good little pet." He kisses my neck, then pushes his thumb inside. "So tight." He alternates rocking his hips and pumping his thumb. "Fuck, you feel good."

Leaning back, he rests his free hand between my shoulder blades and pins me to the bed. His hips work like a well-oiled machine; his cock pounding my pussy while his thumb assaults my ass. I push back into him, silently beg him to give me more. And he rewards me by giving me his whole thumb.

Another thrust and I am in sensation overload. My nipples beg to be pinched. My clit screams to be rubbed. Every nerve ending in my body is on fire. On his next thrust forward, he hits deep and my body detonates. As it does, he continues his assault on both holes and drags out the sensation.

I fist the bedding and cry out against the cotton. "Ohgod, ohgod, ohgod."

He slips his thumb from my hole, fists my hips with a bruising grip and fucks me with abandon. And when I think my body can't take any more, he hits that spot deep inside again and another orgasm swallows me whole. Then his weight is on me, his arm banded around my middle as his release fills me.

"Never leave," he says, breath hot on my back as he squeezes me tighter.

"Can't stay here forever," I tease.

He kisses along my spine. "Lies." When he reaches my mouth, he kisses me with unparalleled tenderness. A bit awkwardly, he slips out of me and lies so we are eye to eye. "Wasn't joking when I said you're mine."

I lower my hips to the mattress and bring a hand to his cheek. "And I believe you. But we just met."

"And?"

"And we know nothing about each other." I laugh. "You may love sex with me, but what if I'm a total psycho?"

"You aren't."

I roll my eyes. "Okay, I'm not." For a moment, I lock eyes with him. Try to read what is going through his head. Unfortunately, I was never great at reading people. "Why the rush?"

"Why wait?"

"Don't you want to know me before I take over your life?"

"I know enough."

I turn onto my side and tuck my hands under my cheek. "How?"

He kisses the tip of my nose. "I'm a good judge of character. Can tell when people try to deceive me. *Hazel.*" He smirks and shakes his head. "I've always been good at it. And now it's part of my job." I arch a brow. "Attorney."

"Okay, I'll give you that."

"Will you now?" he teases. "Anyway, I shared that so you understand why I feel comfortable in my stance."

Although his explanation reassures me, I still think it is

all too soon. We haven't existed around each other a full twenty-four hours yet. What if he hates my day-to-day habits? By no means am I the cleanest person, and Thomas's house, from what I have seen, is pretty damn tidy. What if, weeks from now, he decides I am some annoying girl? He doesn't like the way I squeeze the toothpaste from the tube. Gets frustrated with the way I wash the laundry. Dislikes my eating habits—the leftovers I swear to eat but never do. Then what happens? He throws me aside and moves on.

I have no clue what I want to do with my life; the complete opposite of him. He already has a degree and an adult job. Me? I toss on my blue vest and stand behind the beauty counter at the local drugstore, discussing skincare and cashing out purchases. I make minimum wage and plaster on a fake smile for the masses every day.

How will someone like Thomas—a person with his shit together—stay with a person like me? Simple. He won't.

"Ella?"

I blink away my inward spiral. "Yeah?"

"Whatever you're thinking..." He scoots closer and gives me a chaste kiss. "Please, stop."

Closing my eyes, I take a deep breath. Dig deep for the courage to speak my feelings. If Thomas wants a relationship with me, I need to be able to speak my feelings. Need to voice my fears.

"What if everything is good for weeks, then one day I do something you hate?"

"I doubt that will happen."

"But it could. Then what happens? You throw me out."

Subtly, he shakes his head. "First of all, I'd never throw you out. I'm adult enough to sit down and try to resolve issues. Second, it takes a whole hell of a lot to piss me off. If you have annoying habits—who doesn't, by the way—we'll talk and meet in the middle." He leans in and kisses my shoulder. "That's what couples do, Ella."

"Then why are you single?"

Laughter fills the room. "Maybe you should go into law." I roll my eyes. "I'm single because I never connected with someone the way we connect. I tried. Just didn't work out."

"And you think we will?"

"Without a doubt."

How can this man be so damn sure? His confidence in our future is baffling… and hot as hell. Sure, he is skilled in reading people. But that isn't the same as predicting the future. I want an ounce of his certainty. A snippet of whatever instinct tells him this—us—will work.

With a lick of my lips, I swallow all doubt and take a leap.

"Okay," I whisper.

"Okay?"

I nod. "I want to stay."

Ella directs me through a quaint, single-family homes neighborhood. Navigating us toward her home. Well, her parents' home. Her home is now with me. Yes, the decision was hasty, but I have never felt so sure about anyone.

Every few seconds, I peer in her direction. Notice the way her fingers pick at the hem of her top. I consider asking if she is having second thoughts, but stop myself. We spent hours together talking before getting in the car and driving here.

Her nervousness has nothing to do with me and the move. Her fidgeting fingers and bouncing knee have to do with what awaits her when we enter her parents' home.

Lifting a hand, Ella points to a beige house with forest green trim. A minivan and pickup truck parked in the double driveway. Overall, the house looks ordinary. No plant beds or decorative pieces in the yard. No exterior remodeling to make the 1960s home more current. Just plain colors, a perfectly mowed lawn, and nothing to make others feel welcome.

My poor girl.

I park behind the minivan and we exit the car. We walk toward the front door, hands locked, in a united front. Ella doesn't say a word, but the closer we get to the front door, the tighter she grips my hand. And although I want to tell her everything will be fine, I keep my mouth shut because I know nothing about her life or her parents.

"Ready?" I ask when we step up to the door.

She turns her gaze on me and bites the corner of her lower lip. I hate how worried she is. How antsy she feels. But then she nods and reaches for the doorknob. "Yeah, I think so."

Not five feet in the house, a woman's voice belts out and covers the silence. Her tone sharper than a kitchen knife. "Ella Jean, that better be you." A woman with features similar to Ella, though aged, rounds the corner, stops feet in front of us, and props her hands on her hips. "Where the hell have you been, young lady? Staying out all night without a word." Her gaze shifts as she looks me up and down, a sneer on her lips. "And who might you be?" she asks as her eyes drop to our clasped hands.

"Mama," Ella says, her voice small and frail. "This is Thomas." She looks up and meets my eyes. "My boyfriend."

Ella and I have known each other less than twenty-four hours and I feel as if we are more than boyfriend and girlfriend. We connect on a deeper level. For now, though, I let her explain us in her own words. Her mother doesn't seem the type of woman to listen to much of what Ella says anyway.

"Boyfriend?" she asks incredulously. Then she laughs. Laughs. In front of her daughter. In front of us both. As if Ella being in a romantic relationship is impossible. "Go to your room, young lady." She points down the hall.

Ella starts to move, but I tighten my hold on her. I refuse to let her be a doormat to this woman. She may be her mother, but everyone deserves respect.

"The only way she's going to that room is if she's packing her things to leave," I state firmly.

Ella's mother steps closer. Her lip curled in permanent disgust. "Is that so?"

I will give it to this woman, she is bold and daring. Perhaps this is where Ella's fire comes from. In this situation, though, she needs to back the hell off.

"It is, seeing how Ella is legally an adult."

She rolls her eyes, steps toe-to-toe with me, and jabs a finger in the center of my chest. "Adult or not, she lives under this roof. And until her father and I have a conversation with her about the real world, she's not going anywhere."

Before I rebut the woman's argument, she grabs Ella's free hand and yanks her out of my hold. Ella falls on the floor behind her mother and doesn't move to stand. Behind this woman, Ella looks nothing like the goddess I met last night. And I hate how her parents have crushed her spirit without effort.

"Get out of my house." Her mother points to the door. "Before I call the police."

Ella peeks up from the floor, tears in her eyes. I wait until our stares connect. "I'll be back." Her chin quivers. "I promise."

"If you're smart, you won't," her mother states. "I have the law on speed dial."

My gaze shifts from Ella to her mother. I lean forward, invade her personal space, and smirk. "Yeah? I bet the law I have on speed dial is better."

With that, I spin around, open the door and exit the house. Any second, I might vomit on the lawn — my nerves and anger in overdrive. Leaving without Ella unsettles me in inexplicable ways. Her upbringing and homelife have obviously been nothing short of violent. Hopefully not physically, but definitely emotionally and mentally. If her mother behaved with such cruelty in front of a stranger, I question how she is behind closed doors.

And what about her father? Two vehicles are parked in the driveway. Where was he? Is he the subject of such abuse too? Maybe he doesn't like to get his hands dirty. Or he prefers to keep his misdeeds private.

Regardless, I will rescue Ella from this place. From this wretched life.

Ella is mine. She belongs with me. Safe. Able to stand tall. Be herself. Without subjugation.

Yes, I prefer to be in control. Ella didn't seem to mind

either. But after what just happened, I need to navigate us with a fresh perspective. I need to let her harness the control.

I back out of the driveway, sending a silent message to Ella. *I'll return. Soon.* Then, I drive home and work on a plan on how to do exactly that.

Not only will I return for Ella, but I will leave with her. Because once I step foot on that property again, I refuse to leave without her. Threats and violence may be the tools Ella's mother uses to keep her in line, but she has no idea what I have in my arsenal. Or what I am capable of when pushed too far.

SEVEN

ELLA

A WEEK HAS PASSED since I last saw or spoke with Thomas. Seven very long, torturous days.

When he left, he promised he would return. And I believed—believe—him. Thomas isn't the type of man to make a vow and not hold up his end of the deal. But when he said he would come back, I thought he meant in a day or two.

Maybe he changed his mind. I mean, after how Mother acted toward him, he probably thought I would become a nut job like her. Yes, I may be what some consider abnormal or freakish. But only because the people judging me live in the same circles as my parents. Peers from school were different. Every guy wanted in my pants while every girl either cheered me on or ridiculed my promiscuity.

Only once had my parents learned of my sexual

deviance. I remember the exact moment my mother called me a whore for the first time. Halloween weekend of my sophomore year.

I'd asked my parents if friends could stay the night after we went out and they'd agreed. My friends and I went to a small party at Troy Benson's house—the high school quarterback. There were maybe fifteen of us total, most of them football players. One of the guys brought a couple cases of beer and weed circulated on the regular.

Knowing my parents would be up when we returned home, I didn't partake—much.

At this stage of the game, I'd been sexually active years. The number of partners I'd been with was up there for someone my age, but I was no match for some of the guys' tallies.

An hour into the party, Troy started feeling me up. Out in the open. His fingers dragged up my thigh and under the too-short plaid skirt I wore as part of my costume. He didn't ask, but I didn't tell him to stop. I loved the way guys gravitated toward me. The way they couldn't keep their hands off me. How my body was in control of their needs and urges.

In the middle of his living room, I let Troy Benson finger fuck me. I made no show to disguise what happened. If anything, I put on a show. Knowing the people present comforted me enough to be so vulnerable.

Without words, I invited others to join. And they did. After my first orgasm, other people in the room paired up.

When Troy pushed my skirt up and panties down, then started eating my pussy for all to watch, a few other guys from the team joined us. Within minutes, I was stripped bare and the guys took turns pleasing my body.

Hours later, in the confines of my bedroom, my friends and I whisper-gossiped about the night's events. That is, until my mother burst into the room without knocking. Her face was so red. Her eyes practically bulging from their sockets. Before I asked if everything was okay, she backhanded my cheek.

"Whore!" she shouted loud enough for the neighbors to hear. "You disgust me, Ella Jean. This is not the daughter your father and I raised." I shrunk in her presence and she just kept going. "Out late at a boy's house. Doing unspeakable things with said boy and others." She spit at me. "Have fun with your friends tonight. Because tomorrow, you're grounded. And I'll be speaking with the school about sexual deviancy."

After that night, sex was never discussed with me among my friends. We made a pact. Created our own language of sorts. Months later, my parents finally allowed me to do more than go to school and be at home. Not that I hadn't been fucking guys in bathrooms and closets at school. But I used the guise of tutoring classmates who needed extra help with math or science. Worked every time.

Now, it feels as if I am that fifteen-year-old girl again. Hiding in her room. Trying to figure out a plan to outsmart my parents.

"Ella," my mother calls down the hall. "Dinner."

This pretty much sums up our interaction the last week. Her summoning and me falling in line.

A little longer and this will all be over. Thomas will come back.

And while I waited this past week for his return, I slowly packed my belongings. Only clothes and mementos I wanted to keep. Because no matter what, I am leaving. Even if it is out the damn window in the middle of the night.

I join my parents in the dining room. The room is as arctic as ever, and it has nothing to do with the thermostat setting. I pull out the chair I have sat in my entire life and park myself at the table. Mom sets a plate in front of me with unseasoned chicken cut into bite-sized pieces, plain white rice, overcooked canned carrots, and a slice of white bread with a light coating of butter.

This is how it has always been. Mother controls the house. Although she doesn't cut father's dinner, she portions each of our plates. *"Not too much. I won't buy new clothes because you can't control your appetite."* Father isn't a feeble man. But for some reason, he allows Mother to rule the roost however she pleases.

But I have seen his ugly side too. Been victim of his belt. Heard his malicious words and disturbing grunts as he punished me. Which is why I never provoked my father. Something told me he was capable of things much worse. Nightmare-worthy things.

Outside of this house, people look up to my father. He goes to church, donates to charity, and is a favored entrepreneur in the community. Need someone to look after your business's accounting? Daniel Walsh is the man people refer you to.

To the outside world, my father is a nice man. But I hear him in the night. Watching pornography and jerking himself off while Mother sleeps. I hear him saying dirty things to the actors on screen while he comes in a hand towel. And I hear the women on the screen as they call the men fucking them daddy.

Which is why I will never call my father anything but father.

"Eat your dinner, Ella Jean."

I pick at the food on my plate and silently beg for an extra square of butter or some damn salt and pepper. Would a little parsley kill anyone? No, no it wouldn't.

Staring at my mother, I stab a piece of chicken, bring it to my lips, and eat it. After I swallow, a new fire lights my bloodstream. And for the first time, I voice my opinion to my mother.

"Would it kill you to flavor the food? Maybe some herbs or butter or garlic. We can certainly afford such things."

Clanging fills the air as Mother drops her fork. She stares at me open-mouthed for a beat. A small sense of victory floods beneath my rib cage. Until she slaps my face. Hard.

That will leave a mark.

"How dare you speak to me with such insolence. I am

your mother. You will respect me." She slams her hand on the table. "After everything your father and I have done for you. How dare you disrespect us."

Unable to contain the slow-boil rage bubbling inside, I pop up from my chair. The wood overturns behind me and hits the wall. Heat crawls up my throat and floods my cheeks, amplifying the sting further.

"How dare I?" I ball my fingers into fists. "How dare I?" I shout, letting the fury spill out. "Yes, you are my mother. But I will never respect you. You are the most despicable, two-faced person I know. All prim and proper in front of friends and a cunt behind closed doors."

Mother shoots up from her chair and raises her hand, only this time, I am ready. I catch her hand before it makes contact with my face again. This is the moment my father chooses to stick in his two cents.

"Sally, stop. Obviously, your form of punishment doesn't work. It hasn't worked for years." Father shifts his gaze to me and nausea rolls in my gut. "Time for daddy to punish you."

Bile rises in my throat. I am going to puke.

I drop my mother's hand and step back. "Don't you fucking touch me."

"Been a long time since I took my belt to your ass. Seems time to change that." He rises from his chair and I back myself into the wall. He inches toward me, a predator out in the open, stalking prey.

My eyes drop as he reaches for his belt buckle and

starts unfastening it. I don't miss the bulge beneath his zipper. Vomit hits the back of my throat. Tears sting the backs of my eyes.

No. No, no, no.

He yanks the leather from the loops of his pants with a snarly smile on his lips. Inches from my shrinking frame, vomit fills my mouth. My mother stands behind him with confusion marring her brow and something sinister in her smile.

His hand reaches forward, the leather creaking under his grip. And then the doorbell rings.

Father looks over his shoulder and directs my mother to answer the door. Alone. Redirecting his gaze to me, he assumes my mother did as she was told. Obedient, as always. But she hasn't left the room. Instead, she watches her husband with fresh eyes. Stares after him as he begins pursuit of his only daughter once more.

But he doesn't get far again. The doorbell rings, then rings again, followed by a fist banging the wood.

Red fills father's face before he spins around and storms past Mother. "Guess if *I* need something done around here, I have to do it. Stupid bitch."

Mother stares at me for one, two, three breaths. I see the questions forming on her tongue, but know she won't speak them. Know she won't ask her daughter if her devoted and loving husband has ever *touched* her. Because that would look bad for her.

And I am glad she doesn't ask. Glad she doesn't want

to know the truth. It is sad I don't know if the truth will upset her or relieve her.

Yes, my father has inflicted physical punishment. No, he hasn't sexually assaulted me. I might have killed him in his sleep by now if that were the case.

Finally, she looks away and storms after my father. On slow feet, I follow in their wake. Ready to thank whoever saved me from what would have become my worst nightmare.

I hear them before they come into view. My father and Thomas. The fact that father still has his belt in his hand doesn't look good. Nor does the sneer on his face. Not when three officers stand tall behind Thomas, ready to help me out of this situation.

Thomas looks past my parents and locks my gaze with his. "Ella, are you okay?"

Tears sting the backs of my eyes while a fist tightens around my heart. Years ago, I would have lied and said yes. Because I feared the repercussions of telling the truth, of saying I was not okay. But I am no longer that girl. No longer small. And no one has the right to knock me down. Not even my own flesh and blood.

I shake my head, slowly at first. "No." My head shakes harder. "I am not okay."

With a minor jut of his chin, Thomas signals me away. "Go get your things."

Starting for the hallway, I hear my father shout "she's not going anywhere" as I step inside my room. I hustle to the closet and shoulder the bags I packed and stowed.

After slipping on shoes, I take one last look at my bedroom and take a deep breath.

This is it. This is goodbye. I look up. *Thank you.*

And then I walk out and head toward the future. Toward Thomas.

EIGHT

THOMAS

Three days.

Three days and Ella hasn't talked about what happened at her parents' house. And her silence has me worried.

Her father made it rather evident something was happening when I arrived with the police. Between his red cheeks, angry sneer and the belt in his hand, I feared the worst. When Ella walked off to gather her bags, he put forth his best effort to not let Ella leave. Unfortunately for him, Ella was no longer a minor, nor was she in school, and had every right to leave whenever she pleased. When the police backed me up and not him, this angered him further.

For a moment, I thought he'd start a physical altercation. Thankfully, it didn't come down to that. Not sure I would've restrained myself, even with police present.

Since that night, Ella has crawled inside herself. Much

as I want her to tell me what has her so pensive, I sit in silence and wait. Wait for her mind to settle. Wait for her to come to terms with what happened. And wait for her to know she is safe with me here.

Even in sleep, her brows pinch at the middle, and deep lines mar her forehead. I itch to reach out and smooth the stress away. Instead, I sweep her brilliant-red curls from her cheek and study her soft curves.

The lines shift and smooth as she wakes. Slowly, her eyes open and lock with mine. Cheek propped on my palm, I lie on my side and stare down at her. A small smile adds a soft glow to her skin.

This moment, when her eyes open each day, is my favorite. When life has yet to consume and sway her thoughts. Everything about her in this blip of time is pure and natural and untarnished.

Her arms stretch above her head, back arches, and the sheet slides down her body to expose her bare breasts. Breasts I haven't touched in ten days. Breasts I desperately want to wrap my lips and hands around.

"Morning," I whisper before dropping my lips to hers.

"Hi." The corners of her mouth tip up in a shy smile. "How long have you been awake?"

I trace a knuckle along the line of her jaw. "Not long."

She hums and rolls onto her side, her lips at my throat, breasts pressed to my abs, arm around my waist. I close my eyes and bask in the feel of her body flush with mine. Legs tangled, fingers exploring, breaths hot and heavy.

Fuck, I want to touch her. More than this. More than lazy, soft grazes of skin for mere seconds.

But I won't. Not until she tells me what happened during our time apart. Those seven days were the longest of my life. The look on Ella's face when I arrived says it was more than seven days for her too. Something during those days changed her. Ella isn't the same woman I met. Although she is still physically soft, a piece of her has hardened.

"Thomas?"

I kiss the crown of her head. "Yeah?"

"Did I do something wrong?"

Inching back, I look down at her. Absorb the concern in her eyes. Allow guilt to consume me momentarily, knowing I have acted differently with her. "What makes you think you did?"

Her fingers skirt along my spine and spread at the base to cup my ass. "Because you haven't touched me since I've been back." Before I open my mouth to answer, her hand slides around my hip and dips between my legs. As if second nature, her fingers wrap around my cock. "But this tells me you want to." She presses her lips to the hollow of my throat. "So, why?"

"Ella…" Her name a plea and growl as she strokes my erection, slow and steady. I swallow and close my eyes briefly. "Shouldn't we talk? About what happened."

With a firmer grip, she jerks my cock with more gusto. "No." She releases my cock, pushes against my chest until I am flat on my back, then straddles my hips. "I don't want to talk, Thomas." She strokes the length of my cock with her slick pussy lips. "I want to fuck."

My hands fist her hips in a bruising grip. "We should talk. You can't let it—" I don't get to finish my thought as she glides to the tip of my cock and takes me to the hilt.

"Later," she moans out. She rocks her hips, then slams back down. Our joint moans fill the room. "Right now, I want to fuck you until neither of us can walk." Palms on my pecs, her nails claw my flesh as she glides up and down my cock with desperation. "You can either get on board or lie still and shut up. Either way, I'm fucking you."

This aggressive side of Ella turns me the fuck on… and has me concerned. But I choose to dwell on it later. Right now, my girl needs a good fucking. And her needs will always come first. Always.

We crawl out of bed, literally, and shower the sweat from our skin. After we towel off and dress minimally, I cook us French toast, bacon, eggs, and hash browns. We sit at the dining table, her in an untied robe and me in boxer briefs, and eat our meal.

I stare at her nipples as they peek out of the cotton and lick my lips. Think about her bare pussy as I dunk a piece of French toast in maple syrup. Think about how good she would taste with maple syrup. *Fuck.* At this rate, breakfast will end with her on the table as I pour a trail of syrup from her perky pink nipples to her throbbing clit.

But syrup will have to wait.

Because we need to talk.

I take our plates to the kitchen, rinse them and load them in the dishwasher. Ella comes up from behind and wraps her arms around my waist, kissing the back of my neck. I grab her hands and lift them to my lips. Attempt to soften her before I urge her to talk about a sore subject.

"Ella." I peer over my shoulder and she meets my gaze. "We really should talk."

She huffs and her frame deflates. "Why?"

I spin to face her. Pinch her chin between my thumb and finger. "Because it's not healthy to keep it bottled up." When her eyes drop, I lift her chin. "And I'd rather get it out now than have it fester and become explosive later."

Leaning forward, her arms circle my waist once more. She pulls me impossibly close and rests her cheek where my pec and shoulder meet. I snake my arms around her middle and hold her tight. Minutes pass and neither of us says a word. I grant her the time because she has avoided the subject for a reason. But it is important I know every-thing. She doesn't need to hold all the pain anymore. Now that she has me, I can carry some of her burden too.

"Years ago, when I was fairly young, my father used to punish me with his belt. Over his knee. Bare on my butt." I squeeze her tighter to avoid her seeing the rage boiling my blood. "When you're little, you accept punishments.

You think, *'All the kids must get the same when they're bad.'"* She takes a deep breath and leans back. "Can we sit down?"

I nod, take her hand in mine, and guide us to the couch. Before she sits, I watch as she pulls her robe closed and ties the sash tight. Too tight. The rage in me burns hotter. I hate how broaching the subject makes her shelter herself.

"The first lashing, my mother was present. She approved and wanted to see that I got what they thought I'd deserved. Naturally, after that day, I did everything possible to not get the belt again. Somehow, my father found a reason. My room wasn't clean enough. My grades were not to his standard. I didn't eat all my dinner. I didn't do my chores. The reasons were endless. Mother wasn't around for those punishments, and they felt… different." She inhales deeply. "He never sexually abused me, but it *felt* as if he wanted to."

"Jesus, Ella. Why didn't you tell anyone?"

"I wanted to. But as respected as my parents were, who would've believed me? Plus, he hadn't actually done anything. It was the word of a child against a trusted adult." She toys with the sash of her robe. "Anyway, as I got older, sex entered the equation." My eyes bulge out of the sockets. "Not with my father!" she corrects immediately. "No, with other guys from school. I lost my virginity early and learned how enjoyable sex was." She peers up at me, hesitant. "And sometimes with more than one partner at a time."

A smirk kicks up the corner of my mouth. "That's a different discussion. One I won't discount."

"Good." Then she goes on to tell me all the depraved things she learned about her father and how she avoided being alone with him often. Ella unloads years' worth of strife and anxiety. Gets mountains of hurt and worry off her chest. Unleashes the demons of her past.

And I gladly accept it all. For Ella, I will take as much as she gives. Be her support when she can't hold herself up. Be her anchor when she needs grounding. Our relationship is new and started unconventionally, but from the moment I walked up to Ella, I knew she would be more than a dirty fuck in the middle of a crowd.

Her body sags into the couch when she finishes her story. The green rimming her hazel irises glow a hint brighter. And the tight knot in her robe sash falls away as I tug it free.

"Thank you," I say as I slip off the couch, drop to my knees and situate myself between her legs. She doesn't move, doesn't take a breath, as I spread her knees farther apart. I kiss the inside of her thigh, near her knee, and she gasps. Then I do the same on the opposite side.

"Why are you thanking me?"

My palms trace parallel trails up her thighs and under the robe, pushing the cotton aside and exposing her delicious pink pussy. I place another kiss on each of her thighs, followed by a nip. She jolts in place, but I see the evidence of how it made her feel, glistening between her folds.

"For telling me your story…" Another kiss and bite on her thighs, midway to my end goal. "For trusting me with something so personal." *Kiss, nip. Kiss, nip.* "Fuck, pet. Your trust gets me so damn hard."

"Is that all that gets you hard?" As the last word leaves her lips, she slips a hand between her thighs and strokes her pussy inches from my lips. "Because we can play truth or dare…" Two of her fingers dip inside her cunt. "All." Her slick digits slip out. "Day." Plunge back in. "Every." Back out and move up to circle her clit. "Day."

I spread her legs as far as they will go. Don't take my eyes off her fingers as they toy with her clit and fuck her cunt. Don't move to touch her or taste her. I simply sit frozen, my mouth a breath from her sweet pussy and watch my girl finger fuck herself.

Her whimpering cries fill the air as her orgasm nears. She tries to close her legs, but I pin them in place. Leave her exposed and soaked and glorious. Her fingers rub her clit faster, harder, as she edges closer. Then she dips them back in her cunt, two fingers, then three, and pumps faster, pushes deeper.

"That's a pretty little pet. Look how pretty that pussy is. So wet and pink and hungry." My eyes lock on hers. "Feed that pussy what it wants, pet. Fuck it hard. Stroke it how it feels good and show me. Come on your fingers. Do it for me."

I watch as she strokes and fucks herself. Listen as her cries grow closer and louder. Bask in the sight of her as red blotches pattern her skin and she finally lets go. Rip her hand away and eat her raw as she continues to orgasm on my face.

"Such a beautiful pet," I say as I rock back on my heels and trace her pussy with my finger. "Now, I will reward you. Fuck you on the couch like a good little pet."

THE FIRST TIME I met Thomas's coworkers, I mentally prepared myself for judgment and criticism. Without effort, it was easy to see I was younger than Thomas. Not to mention the fact that I looked younger than my actual age. The side-glances from strangers at stores and in public places didn't go unnoticed. Anytime I spoke up, Thomas shrugged it off. Told me to ignore it. That the opinions of others didn't matter.

Although his words repeated in my head, I prepared myself for the worst with his coworkers. But the judgment never came. Neither did the occasional stare or unspoken questions in their expressions.

It was a challenge to accept that not every person was cruel, that not every person will look at you with a critical eye. As part of the healing process, I remind myself each day, not every person is Sally or Daniel Walsh.

Tonight is the annual fundraiser for Thomas's firm.

Everyone is here and dressed to the nines. Hundreds of guests mingle among the firm employees, chatting over wine and hors d'oeuvres. Ready to fork over thousands of dollars to a charitable cause.

Amazing as it all is, it boggles my mind that this is my life. That I occasionally wear fancy dresses, always have the most handsome man on my arm, and talk about money as if this is Monopoly and I have a stockpile.

Someone pinch me. Or don't.

A little more than six months ago, I was just another random woman in a filthy, deserted warehouse. Abandoned by her friend. Next to some random pervert on a couch watching other people have sex. Then, Thomas stepped in front of me, offered his hand, and stole my heart.

Our relationship is still young and we are exploring so much—of ourselves, and with others. I have zero doubts about our future, but I can't wait to see where it leads us.

"You are ravishing in that dress," Thomas whispers in my ear. "Can't wait to peel it off you."

"Is that so?" I cock a brow.

"Indeed."

I scan the room, take in the crowd and gauge how much time we have before the auction begins. "What if I said you should see what's underneath now?"

Thomas clamps onto my hip and bruises the flesh beneath the silk. "Then I'd say you're a naughty little pet." He shifts his hand to mine and hauls me from the banquet hall. We scurry down the wide corridor toward the restrooms. "Wait here." Thomas disappears inside the men's room for three rapid breaths before opening the door and yanking me inside. "In there. Now."

I bolt into the stall and he follows me in. The nice thing about upscale venues… the bathroom stall walls are floor to ceiling and the stalls are more spacious.

Thomas puts the lid down on the toilet and pushes me down. He unbuttons and unzips his slacks, shoves his briefs down, and fists his cock. Swiping the tip over my lips, he pushes his way in. "Suck me like a good little pet."

Without resistance, I do as he says. I swirl my tongue around the length of his cock and suck the tip on each pass. He fists the hair at the nape of my neck, tips my head back slightly, and thrusts forward until his balls slap my chin.

"Such a good little pet." He strokes my cheek with his other hand. "Are you wet for me, pet?"

I mumble my yes around his girth and choke when he pushes harder.

"Show me. Push your dress up and show me how wet you are." Finagling my dress while sucking his cock, I shove it above my hips and expose my bare pussy. Thomas clucks his tongue. "No panties at the party." He pulls his cock from my lips. "Naughty, naughty pet."

Slipping his hands under my arms, he hauls me upright. Then he spins me around and slaps my ass. Before a yelp leaves my lips, the main door to the bathroom opens and someone steps in. Thomas hikes my dress up, leans forward, and whispers in my ear.

"Not a peep, my pet. Unless you want me to watch you with another man tonight." I shake my head. "Good pet."

Then Thomas fills my cunt with his cock. I gasp without sound. He fucks me hard and fast in the stall, and part of me wonders if he wants the other man in the room to hear us. Wonders if he wants someone else to fill me while he watches. We both get off on it—watching each other as we fuck other people. It is more about the act than anything else.

Thomas and I are solid. Bonded like no other. He is mine and I am his. No one fucks me like him. No one loves me like he does. And he would say the same in regard to me. But we love when others join us, play with us, evoke pleasure within us. It keeps the spark between us alive and electric and fresh.

The sink in the bathroom turns on and Thomas picks up his pace. His balls slap my clit and I can't stop the guttural moan that slips out. He grabs my throat to silence me, but I know it is too late. No doubt, we have been heard.

A soft knock raps our stall door, but Thomas doesn't stop.

"All good in there?" the man says, his voice rough and vaguely familiar.

Thomas cracks the door and I look over my shoulder to see Brad, one of the guys who came to the club with him six months ago. I didn't know this fact until recently, not until Thomas told him about me, about us.

"Yeah, man. So fucking good," Thomas says as he slows his rhythm and lets Brad watch. "You good?"

Brad fists his cock in his pants and licks his lips as he watches us fuck. "Not as good as you."

Thomas peeks out the door. "We alone?"

"Absolutely."

"Go in the handicap stall." Thomas pulls out of me and lowers my dress. "C'mon pet. Time to play."

We follow Brad into the new stall and lock the door. It isn't long before Thomas fucks me from behind again while I suck Brad off. The pace is slow and steady and everything I want from my life with Thomas. Being in this position, taking two men, having two men *want* me, makes me powerful. A goddess. A queen in my own right.

Brad fucks my throat until his cum warms my belly. Thomas fucks my cunt and fills my ass with his thumb until my body can't handle any more and I let go. Not only am I sated, but I feel high on life. A high no drug would provide.

Brad exits the stall and restroom first, checks the coast is clear, then Thomas and I exit. As we walk back to the party, we make tentative plans to have Brad over at the house in the near future.

When we reenter the party, no one is aware of the debauchery that just went down. Part of me wants everyone to know, wants everyone to watch. But another part of me revels in the secrecy of it all. The lewdness and raw nature of who we are. Thomas doesn't degrade or punish me for who I am. Instead, he helps me love who I am. Teaches me it is okay to have these urges. It is okay to fuck other people, as long as he approves and is present. It is okay to be my true self.

Thomas makes me whole. Allows me to embrace my sexuality. Encourages me to show him what I want and who I want. And I love that he stands right beside me each day. Never overstepping. Always supportive. He fulfills my needs and I do the same in return.

Our love may not be conventional, but it is ours. An impenetrable force.

This is why Thomas will always be mine and I will always be his. Because we truly understand who we are, as individuals and as a couple.

"I love you," I tell him as I lean back and mold myself to his front.

His arms snake around my waist and hug me impossibly close as he kisses beneath my ear. "I love you too, pet."

EPILOGUE

THOMAS

November 7 – Two years later

TOOK way too fucking long for this day to arrive, but today is finally here. Today, and every day going forward, Ella Walsh will be Ella Reynolds. My fucking wife. Queen. Goddess of my soul.

I didn't need a notarized piece of paper to tell the world Ella is mine. But I wanted it anyway. Wanted to connect us in every possible way. Legally seems the last way on the list.

Can't say I ever envisioned this day before Ella entered my life. My wedding day.

Before Ella, sex was just sex. Nothing substantial. A means to an end. An act to fulfill a primal need. No woman made me want more than a quick fuck. Until Ella. Before her, sex was always quick and dirty. Don't get me wrong, we have our share of fast fucks. I love quickies in bathrooms or bushes or alleys. But I have grown to love the slow and lewd moments too. Savoring each touch and stroke and moan. How I make her feel. How she makes me feel.

With Ella, everything is precise and clear. She feeds my primal urges as well as my soul. Gives life more definition. More significance. Couldn't imagine a better existence without her.

So, when she asked to have the glamorous wedding dress and big shindig, I caved without resistance.

I would have been content doing things at the courthouse; keeping things short, sweet, and to the point. But that isn't what my girl wanted. She has given me so much of herself, it is only fair I return the favor. If a gorgeous gown and saying our I dos in front of a crowd was on her wish list, then that is my gift to her.

Ella doesn't ask for much, but when she does, I never refuse her. Our wedding is far from a grand affair, but the event is big to us. Considering our form of celebration doesn't match the "typical" standard, our wedding is the most exposed we have been with people who don't know our… tastes.

That celebration is saved for later.

Four months ago, when I proposed to Ella, we celebrated for hours at home. Fucked on every surface of the living room until we were boneless. Then, I took her to our favorite place in the city. Provocateur. A small sex club hidden under the guise of a strip bar—you just had to know the right person and where to go.

We watched for hours before I told Ella to pick. Like my girl always did, she chose a couple. Although she loved dominating two men at once, every now and again, she loved the tenderness of a woman. We'd stripped bare and fucked in Provocateur until the doors locked at two in the morning. Then we invited the couple to our home and partied until sunrise.

Dominic and Chloe became quick friends with me and Ella after that night. Aside from the occasional hookup, we did things together like normal couples. Hanging out, dinner, movies, mini golf. And today, they sit in the crowd of less than fifty to celebrate our wedding.

A wedding that starts any minute.

Although she wanted the big dress and party, we kept the wedding ceremony simple. I didn't want her to worry about who would walk her down the aisle since her father was out of the equation. So, we opted for no groomsmen or bridesmaids. No flower girl or ring bearer. Just her, me, the ordained minister, and our guests.

The soft lilt of Pachelbel's "Canon in D" floats through the air and the banquet room falls silent. I clasp my hands at my waist, take a deep breath and wait for the doors to open. When they do, all air leaves my lungs.

"Fuck," I mutter as she comes into view.

I never thought it possible for Ella to steal my breath more than before. And I have never been more wrong in my life.

Crisp white lace hugs every inch of her frame from bust to knees before the skirt flows loosely and dusts the floor, a small train in her wake. Flesh-colored fabric beneath the lace alludes to exposed skin while thin spaghetti straps meet the deep V bust and accentuate Ella's full breasts. Her brilliant-red locks hang in loose waves, framing her face and dusting her breasts. A red and white bouquet of calla lilies and roses clasped in her hands.

I snap mental pictures of this moment while the photographer and our friends capture images for print. For as long as I live, I want this moment imprinted on my heart and embedded in my soul. The day Ella walks down the aisle to be my wife.

A few strides past the front row of guests and Ella stands across from me. Unable to resist, I lean forward and kiss her cheek. "You are stunning," I whisper for her ears only. When I resume my position, I note the blush pinking her complexion. "Stunning," I mouth.

Then, the minister kicks off her part of the ceremony.

ELLA

Monday through Friday, I am blessed to see Thomas in a suit. Sharp and classic and mouthwatering. Thomas, in a suit, is my kryptonite. But Thomas in *this* suit will be my undoing.

As the minister talks about finding your other half and what it means to love another person, I rake my libidinous eyes up and down Thomas.

The stylish black suit with a muted plaid pattern hugs Thomas's trim frame. Beneath the suit jacket is a charcoal-gray vest, crisp white dress shirt, and a burgundy tie; a matching handkerchief in the breast pocket of his jacket. A black belt and dress shoes pull the ensemble together.

My mouth salivates as I clamp my thighs together. One look in Thomas's mossy-green eyes, he knows exactly where my thoughts are.

"Soon," he mouths before the corner of his lips kick up.

Yes, soon. Preferably in the dressing room before the reception. Ten to fifteen minutes of Thomas taking his wife for the first time. Claiming me with a new label. Husband.

And waiting for the reception to end… that may be its own form of torture. Knowing I would be on edge, that waiting would be agony, I preemptively booked the reception for the shortest time frame possible without it appearing odd to our guests.

Thomas didn't know yet, but I had delicious plans for later.

After we exchange vows and I dos, Thomas kisses me as if no one is in the room. We break apart to cheers and applause. As the crowd exits the room and heads for a larger space several doors down for the reception, I haul Thomas into the dressing room.

"As stunning as you are in that dress, I want to tear it off you," he says as the lock clicks into place.

"Time for that later." I saunter to where he stands near

the door, palming his dick. "Right now, husband" —he groans— "you need to take care of your wife."

He steps into me, brushes his knuckles along my jaw. "I will always take care of you, wife. Always." His lips meet mine in a hungry kiss. "No one is more important than you."

I peel the spaghetti straps from my shoulders and push my dress to the floor. Clad in a nude garter belt, stockings, a garter and nothing more, I squeeze his cock through the fabric and drop to my knees. Making quick work of his belt, I undo his slacks and shove them down. Followed by his briefs. His cock springs free and I lick my lips, eager to taste him.

"You want to suck me off, pet?"

Peering up at him, I lick the tip of his cock. "I want you in my throat before you fuck my cunt, husband."

He growls and cups my jaw. "Then take what you want, wife. Take what belongs to you."

And I do, until he retreats, yanks me up from my knees and spins me around. With time of the essence, he slams into me and pistons his hips. Works my body religiously until we both climax. Until our bones are jelly. He leaves a trail of kisses from beneath my ear to the edge of my shoulder as we catch our breaths.

Ever the gentleman, Thomas helps me back into my dress. Kisses me possessively one last time. Then we exit the dressing room with heated skin and glowing smiles. Enter the reception, greet our guests, and celebrate our love for each other with close friends and family.

When I walked into the underground party a little more than two years ago, I never expected to leave with my future husband. But I did.

The first night with Thomas felt fantasy-like. Yes, I was reluctant to have sex with a stranger for all to see. But then I took my first real breath after a lifetime of being suffocated. And I let my desires take over. Unbeknownst to him, Thomas fulfilled my depraved needs. Made me feel safe and whole and more myself.

Thomas not only embraces my darkest fantasies, he encourages them. There is no jealousy or misplaced trust. Since the moment we met, there has been nothing but honesty between us. Some truths were more challenging and took more strength to reveal, but every piece of our pasts is exposed. Nothing and no one will come between us or sever our bond.

Thomas Reynolds is more than my lover and husband. He is the key to my heart, the missing piece of my soul, and the king of my lechery. And I will spend the rest of forever giving him what he needs. Fulfilling our darkest impulses as his devoted wife and naughtiest pet.

Nine years later

"Almost ready?"

I lean against the frame of the bathroom door and watch Ella as she applies nude gloss to her lips. Take a deep breath and admire my radiant wife. No matter how much time passes, she still manages to make me breathless and weak in the knees.

"Ready." She screws the lid on her gloss and stows it in her clutch.

Since Ella and I married, not much has changed. The fire between us is still explosive. The desire to have others in our bed is still as imperative. That said, things are also different.

Over the years, Ella and I have become more selective and careful about who we invite into our bed. All it takes is one bad experience to shift the way you live. Unfortunately for us, we encountered the wrong person four years ago. A man we invited into our home and revealed our most private selves to. In turn, he became our worst nightmare.

Dozens of phone calls to each of us daily. Unannounced appearances at our front door and places we visited. Notes on my car and Ella's in the middle of the day. Breaking into our house when we weren't home and masturbating on our bed—all caught on camera after I installed home security.

Needless to say, the man was arrested. For an extra layer of precaution, for when he is released from jail, restraining and trespass orders were filed. Orders don't always keep people away, but they make the repercussions of violation more substantial.

The experience frightened us both and we have changed tactics on how we move forward with new people.

I proffer my elbow to Ella and she takes it without hesitation. "Stunning as always." I kiss her temple and guide us out of the house and to the car. "Are you excited for tonight?" I start the car and reverse out of the driveway.

"Yes. I talked to Chloe the other day and she said the place is unlike any other."

Through hours of research and talking with friends who share our same lifestyle, I learned the same about Boundless—a new, exclusive sex club in the area. Boundless isn't like the days of grungy secret sex parties or hole-in-the-wall clubs with disco lights and sticky seats. Boundless requires an invitation, hefty membership fees and approval by the owner and management who understand the life and our need for a private, safe place to be ourselves.

Our first visit tonight isn't about leaving with another person or couple. Tonight is about getting a lay of the land and determining how comfortable we are in a new place. Boundless may be upscale and exclusive, but that doesn't necessarily mean it is the right fit for us.

I park the car in the lot for Opulence, the ritzy restaurant housed above Boundless and owned by the same man. He owns a similar setup not far from here—The Sophisticate, a luxury bar, and P.I., the premier, members-only strip club downstairs. Ella and I visited The Sophisticate weeks ago and were invited into P.I. for the evening. It was quite the experience. Before we left, Rocco, the owner, extended memberships to one or both clubs. We were more keen on Boundless than P.I., but jumped at the opportunity.

An exclusive place to be ourselves without grotesque perverts invading our comfort zone.

We enter Opulence and approach the host stand. I give the young woman our reservation details and she guides us to our table. Dinner is elegant and delicious and perfect. The mood of the restaurant relaxing and delightful. After I pay the tab, I show the server our membership card for Boundless and he juts his chin toward the back of the restaurant. A pleasant smile on his face, he wishes us a good evening and walks off.

Rising from the chair, I hold out my hand for Ella. "Shall we?"

She slips her hand in mine as her chair slides back and she stands tall. "We shall."

Hand in hand, we head for the back of the restaurant and toward two very beefy men guarding the roped-off stairwell. Producing our membership cards and identification, they compare the two to a list on a tablet. They hand back the cards, unhook the rope, step aside and tell us to enjoy ourselves.

The farther we descend the stairs, the more the music vibrates the walls and our bones. Soft lighting illuminates the stairwell and corridor. Carnal energy inhabits the walls. Then the corridor ends and Boundless comes into view.

A sensual glow about the space from the industrial Edison bulbs around the club. The walls dark yet warm. An expansive bar consumes most of the right wall and ends near the roped-off VIP section. Past VIP and beyond are poles, cages, suspension grids, padded tables and an array of implements.

Past the instruments, I spot numbered doors. If memory serves, Rocco said those are private rooms for those not into exhibitionism. Although, some of the rooms have two-way mirrors for those who want to try exhibitionism without seeing the voyeurs. Leather couches, chairs and various other pieces of furniture sporadically fill the club. Lit candles at the center of the tables and usable in play.

Boundless is much more than I expected. More pristine and attractive and tempting than I pictured in my mind's eye. This place smells of leather and amber and freedom. A scene where being our true selves is welcomed and encouraged.

I tug Ella closer to my side and bring my lips to her ear. "What do you think?"

After a deep breath, she twists her profile and brings us face to face. A breath apart, her eyes meet mine. "Feels like home."

"Indeed it does."

We step up to the bar and order drinks. The bartender informs us our membership includes access to VIP, which I knew. The upcharge on top of membership was worth the price. Unsure what we'd walk into, I wanted the opportunity to separate us from the crowd, if need be. Being our first night here, I'd rather we observe from the quieter area of the club. Once we feel comfortable, Ella and I will explore all that Boundless has to offer.

Entering VIP, Ella steers us to a couch next to a lone woman. She sits tall in a throne-like leather chair, poised and observant, as she sips a glass of wine. Russet curls frame her face and glasses. And there is something about her, something I can't quite place, that has both Ella and I homing in on her.

Taking a seat, Ella greets the woman and introduces

us. "Good evening. I'm Ella and this is my husband, Thomas."

"Welcome," she says as if she knows this is our first visit. "Christy." She points across the room to a man with similar stature to myself. But that is where the physical similarities end. "And that's Rick, my boyfriend and one of the club managers."

Well, that little tidbit just made me ten times more comfortable.

Ella and Christy chat while I sit back and observe. Take note of Ella's comfort level with this new woman. Watch their body language and pick up minor details of their conversation. Any time we meet someone new, someone who may be of interest, this is one of many steps in my process. Checking Ella's ease with them. Her level of comfort matters more than anything.

By all accounts thus far, Ella and Christy are two peas in a pod. More at ease with each other than Ella is with Chloe, which is saying something.

Rick enters VIP, kisses Christy, introduces himself and takes a seat.

Without effort, we converse about life and work. Discuss our sexual preferences and the places we have frequented in the past. And it isn't long before I randomly start my standard list of questions. Rick and Christy answer and he asks his own questions. Neither come across as arrogant or blunt, and neither of us states the fact we are interviewing the other as potentials for more outside these walls.

On all accounts, I feel safe near Rick and Christy. And with the occasional glance from Rick, I am also more aroused by a man than ever.

May need to call Dominic when we leave. Not that Ella will mind.

Minutes turn into hours as we chat. Rick had to walk off for work but has since returned. When closing time approaches, Ella and Christy exchange phone numbers. That is her way of stating she wants to pursue more. Years ago, we would have asked them to come back to our place on night one. Would have had them in our bed shortly after passing the threshold.

Now, we vet people and get to know them. Become friends, to some degree, before bedmates. When women are involved, Ella typically starts the process.

We rise and say our goodbyes. As we exit the club, I kiss Ella's temple. "Did you have a nice time?"

She hugs me closer to her frame. "I did." We ascend the stairs and step past the guards. "Is it just me or did Christy and Rick feel... right?"

Exiting the restaurant, we weave through the parking lot and I open the car door for her. When I join her, I swivel in my seat and take her hand, kissing her knuckles in turn. "Not just you." I reach out and tug at the end of her red locks. "Get to know her. If you want more, and so do they, then we'll move forward. Say the word."

Leaning across the console, Ella presses her lips to mine. "Thank you."

"For what?"

"Always loving me for me."

"I wouldn't want you any other way, pet."

A soft smile plumps her cheeks. "Good." Then she removes my hand from her hair and brings it between her thighs. Fire lights her green-rimmed hazels. "Now, take me home and fuck me."

I slip my hand under her dress, scoot her panties to the side, and dip my finger in her cunt. Her moan fills the car as I pump in and out. "I have a better idea."

She hikes up the skirt, spreads her legs, and rocks her hips. "I love when you have better ideas."

I start the car and wait for my phone to connect. Fingers still thrusting, I press a button on the steering wheel. "Call Dominic." Ella groans.

He picks up on the second ring. "What's up, T?"

Ella's pants and soft whimpers fill the car. No doubt he hears them too. "Busy?"

"Nothing that can't wait until later," he says, voice gruffer. A tone change I know all too well. "Mine or yours?"

"Yours. Fifteen minutes?"

"See you in fifteen."

The call disconnects and I pull my fingers away. Ella's cry of disappointment fills the car, but vanishes when I switch hands. "Have to drive, pet. Put your seat belt on and keep those pretty legs spread." I pull out of the lot and drive toward Dominic's place. "Tell me something, pet."

"Anything," she says as I circle her clit.

"Do you want to taste Christy?" Her moan fills the car. "Put your lips on her cunt."

"God, yes."

My middle and ring finger fill her cunt, pumping a vicious rhythm. "Do you want to feel Rick's thick cock in your pussy?"

"Yes," she moans out.

"Do you want to watch me fuck them too?"

"Please," she begs.

"Such a good little pet." A mile from Dominic and Chloe's house, Ella comes on my fingers and all over the seat. I suck her juices off my digits and moan as I park the car. "If you want to start something with Christy and Rick, enjoy your time here tonight. It may be our last."

She rubs her thighs together as she unbuckles her belt. "I will."

"And Ella?"

"Yes?"

"I love you." I lean forward and kiss her. "Always."

"I love you, too." She squeezes her thighs once more. "Now escort me inside and please your wife."

"Yes, ma'am."

Have you read Christy and Rick's steamy, secret life

romance, Undying Devotion? Dive into their steamy suspense today.

Find out why Tiffany hesitates to say yes when Liz proposes Beloved Devotion. How well does she really know the woman she loves?

Distorted Devotion

Swept off her feet by love, life takes a dark, unexpected turn. Now the love of her life may be the cause of her death. Check out this gripping, romantic suspense.

Undying Devotion

A long-term couple with a secret life. Their friends envy the bond they share, but remain oblivious to their lifestyle and how deep the bond lies. A turn of events has her wanting to spill every secret.

Beloved Devotion

She asks the love of her life to marry her. When her girlfriend hesitates, then says yes, she is determined to learn why. As the pieces start to fall in place, she discovers she doesn't know her fiancée at all.

The Click Duet

High school sweethearts torn apart. When fate gives them a second chance, one doesn't trust they won't be hurt again. Through the Lens (Click Duet #1) and Time Exposure (Click Duet #2) is an angsty, second chance, friends to lovers romance with all the feels.

The Insomniac Duet

He was her high school bully. She was the outcast that secretly crushed on him. More than ten years later, he's her boss, completely oblivious to their shared past, and wants no one but her. More importantly, he doesn't understand her animosity toward him.

Depths Awakened

A small town romance which captivates you from the start. Two broken souls have sworn off love. Vowed to never lose anyone else. But their undeniable attraction brings them together and refuses to let go.

Transcendental

A musician in search of his muse and a woman grieving the loss of her husband. Two weeks at an exclusive retreat and their connection rivals all others. Until she leaves early without notice. But he refuses to give up until he finds her again.

Ink Veins

Persephone Autumn's debut poetry collection, Ink Veins, explores topics of depression, love, and self-discovery with a raw, unfiltered voice.

Broken Metronome

When the music of the heart dies…

Broken Metronome is an angsty poetry collection full of heartache and the possibility of what may have been.

THANK YOU

Thank you so much for reading **Darkest Devotion,** a Devotion Series Novelette. If you wouldn't mind taking a moment to leave a review on the retailer site where you made your purchase, Goodreads and/or BookBub, it would mean the world to me.

Reviews help other readers find and enjoy the book as well.

Much love,
    Persephone

Connect with Persephone

www.persephoneautumn.com

Subscribe to Persephone's Newsletter

www.persephoneautumn.com/newsletter

Join Persephone's Reader Group

Persephone's Playground

Follow Persephone Online

instagram.com/persephoneautumn

facebook.com/persephoneautumnwrites

tiktok.com/@persephoneautumn

goodreads.com/persephoneautumn

bookbub.com/authors/persephone-autumn

amazon.com/author/persephoneautumn

pinterest.com/persephoneautumn

twitter.com/PersephoneAutum

ACKNOWLEDGMENTS

Thank you to my family and friends for you constant support. Writing books is a lonely job, but you cheer me on every step of the way. Not to mention all the book pimping.

Thank you to Ellie McLove, my kick ass editor, and Rosa Sharon, the best fairy proof mother, at *My Brother's Editor*. Just when I think I have the punctuation down, you prove me wrong. You not only correct too many commas in each story, you also give me valuable insight on how to make my book babies better. You ladies are rockstars!

Thank you for this stunning cover, Abi! Your artistry makes my heart oh so happy!

Thank you author friends. Author life can be rough at times. I am so grateful to have so many of you in my life. I hope we all get to squeeze each other one day.

Thank you to the readers and bloggers that continue to choose my books. Before I first pressed publish, my goal was to sell at least one copy of my book to someone I didn't know. In the grand scheme of things, I'm still a baby author, but I appreciate you all more than words will express.

Thank you Abigail Davies, for reaching out to me to join the Coerced Anthology. Although they were pre-made covers, you designed my first romance and non-romance. Not only do you create brilliant covers, you also write fabulous stories and have the biggest heart.

And if this is the first book of mine you've read… thank you for taking a chance on my book. I hope you enjoyed it and will stick around.

ABOUT THE AUTHOR

Persephone Autumn lives in Florida with her wife, crazy dog, and two lover-boy cats. A proud mom with a cuckoo grandpup. An ethnic food enthusiast who has fun discovering ways to veganize her favorite non-vegan foods. If given the opportunity, she would intentionally get lost in nature.

For years, Persephone did some form of writing; mostly journaling or poetry. After pairing her poetry with images and posting them online, she began the journey of writing her first novel.

She mainly writes romance and poetry, but on occasion dips her toes in other works. Look for her non-romance publications under P. Autumn.